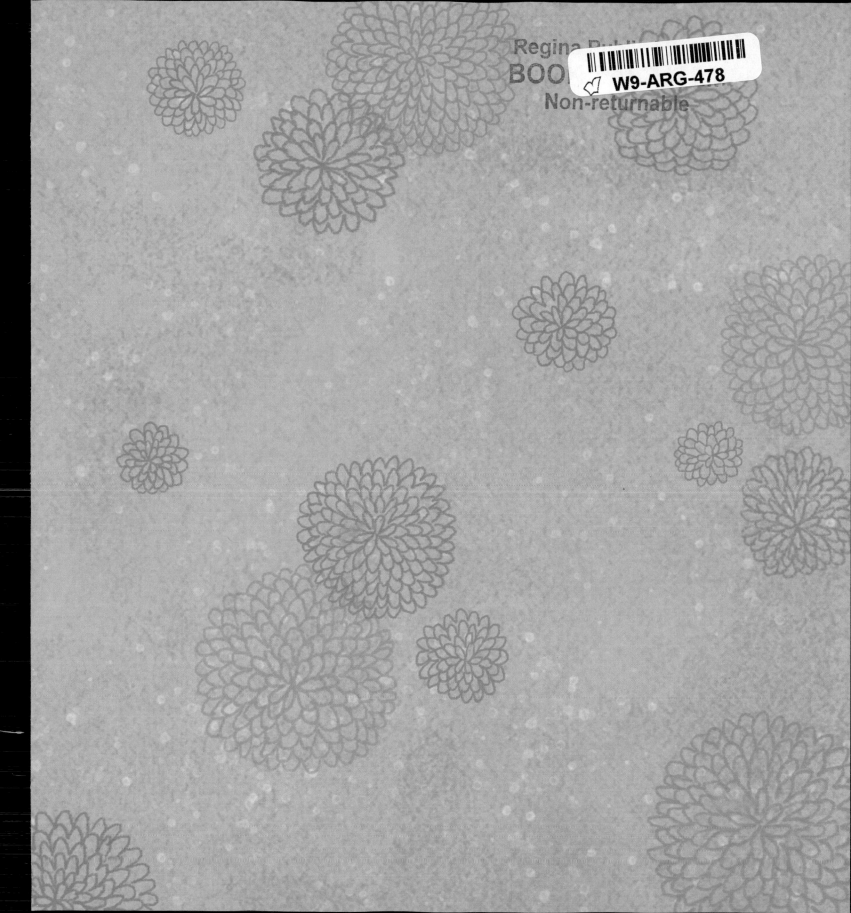

W9-ARG-478

Groundwood Books / House of Anansi Press
groundwoodbooks.com

We acknowledge for their financial support of our publishing program the
Canada Council for the Arts, the Ontario Arts Council and the Government
of Canada.

  Canada Council   Conseil des Arts
for the Arts   du Canada

ONTARIO ARTS COUNCIL
CONSEIL DES ARTS DE L'ONTARIO
an Ontario government agency
un organisme du gouvernement de l'Ontario

With the participation of the Government of Canada
Avec la participation du gouvernement du Canada | Canadä

Library and Archives Canada Cataloguing in Publication
Quan, Betty, author
Grandmother's visit / Betty Quan ; [illustrated by] Carmen Mok.
Issued in print and electronic formats.
ISBN 978-1-55498-954-6 (hardcover). — ISBN 978-1-55498-955-3 (PDF)
I. Mok, Carmen, illustrator II. Title.
PS8583.U332G73 2018   jC813'.54   C2018-900043-0
C2018-900044-9

The illustrations were painted digitally.
Design by Michael Solomon
Printed and bound in Malaysia

 MIX
Paper from
responsible sources
FSC® C012700
FSC
www.fsc.org

In memory of Sheila Koffman
and Sheila Barry. — BQ

For Sheila Barry and
Michael Solomon, thank you
for your trust in me.
For Wing Pak, thank you for
your endless support. — CM

Grandmother's Visit

Betty Quan   Pictures by Carmen Mok

GROUNDWOOD BOOKS
HOUSE OF ANANSI PRESS
TORONTO BERKELEY

My grandmother teaches me the secret
of measuring rice to water.
    She presses her fingertip against the
surface of the rice and adds enough
water to reach the first joint.

My grandmother tells me about when she was a girl growing up in China.

On special occasions, the children of her village were treated to red lotus beans boiled in sugar and served cold, with ice.

Grandmother is always
savoring the flavors of her
childhood. I like her stories.
They taste salty and sweet, like
the pickled plums Grandmother
hides in her pockets.

Every morning, my mother and father go to work, and Grandmother walks me to school. Every morning, Grandmother and I say goodbye.

After school,
Grandmother and
I say hello. We walk
home together.

I help Grandmother make dinner. I like washing
the rice until the water becomes so clear you can see
every tiny white grain.

Grandmother remembers when she was a little girl just like me. Her fingers were too small to measure the water, so she would dip her braid in until the water reached her ribbon.

Grandmother sometimes forgets to take her house key with her when she goes out.

Mother makes Father put a hook for it in Grandmother's bedroom. Whenever she reaches for her dark blue quilted jacket, she can see the house key next to it.

One day, Grandmother stops walking me to school and back. Every day now, Father leaves work early to come get me at school. He makes us dinner. Nobody is ever hungry. The rice bowls stay full.

Grandmother's door is always closed.
Mother and Father are always whispering.

One day, Grandmother's room is empty. Her
comb and jade bracelet sit on her dresser.

Her photo album rests on the table, next to
the bed she no longer sleeps in.

Her dark blue quilted jacket now hangs in the
closet. No more pickled plums are hidden
in its pockets.

And Grandmother's house key
remains on its hook.

A few days later, my
grandmother is buried.

That night, Mother turns on all our outside lights.

Mother tells me that some Chinese people believe you should turn on the outside lights after someone has died. Then the spirit of the dead person can find their way back home. Through all the darkness. So they can say one final goodbye.

The world outside is still and quiet. So is the room across the hall from mine.

Grandmother's room.

My ears strain to remember the sound of her voice. To hear her stories. To hear her laughter.

Instead, I hear something else. The jangle of a key against a jade key ring.

When I go into Grandmother's room, I see that her house key is no longer on its hook. I find the key inside Grandmother's photo album, like a bookmark. There is a picture of my grandmother holding a little baby on her lap.

The baby is me.

Hello.

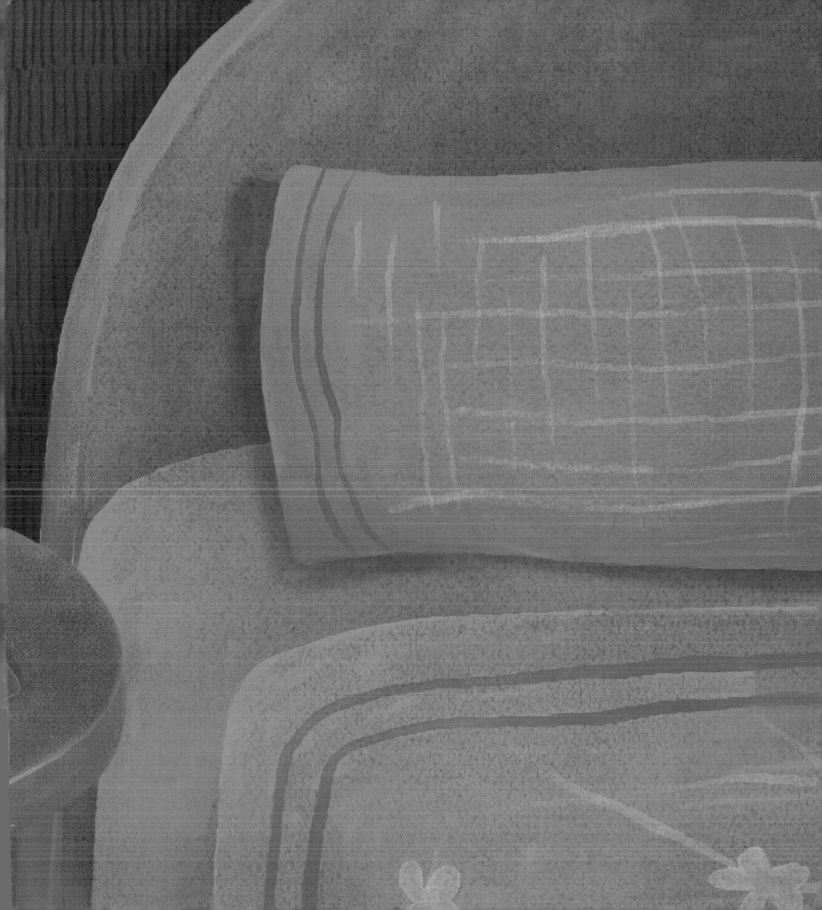

My grandmother taught me the secret of measuring rice to water.

My grandmother told me about when she was a girl growing up in China.

Tonight, my grandmother came to tell me, Goodbye.

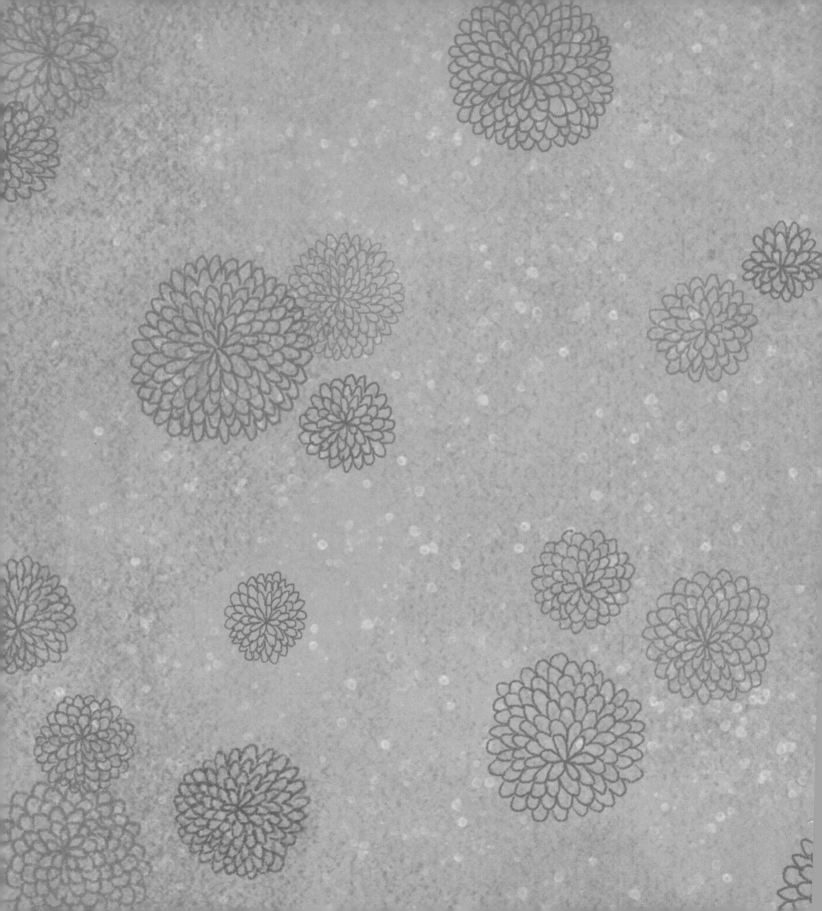